POEMS OF

selected by Jack Prelutsky

DRAGONFL,
ALFRED A. KNOPF

A. Nonny Mouse.

ILLUSTRATED by Henrik Drescher

ooks
New York

A DRAGONFLY BOOK PUBLISHED BY ALFRED A. KNOPF, INC.

Compilation, introduction, ''A Silly Young Fellow Named Ben,'' ''I Dribbled
Catsup on My Pet,'' ''A Clever Gorilla Named Gus,'' and ''The Farm Is in a
Flurry'' copyright © 1989 by Jack Prelutsky
Illustrations copyright © 1989 by Henrik Drescher

Library of Congress Catalog Card Number: 89-31672
ISBN: 0-679-81996-7
First Dragonfly Books edition: September 1991

Manufactured in the United States of America 10 9 8 7 6 5 4 3 2

For Edward and Susanna Gonzales

J. P.

For Uli and Lauren

H. D.

Introduction

One morning several years ago there was a letter in my mailbox from a Ms. A. Nonny Mouse, with whom I was not previously acquainted. It was written in a charming and light-hearted manner, and I could tell at once that A. Nonny Mouse was no ordinary rodent. Her wit was far more clever than one might expect from a creature with no chin, sparse fur, and a long, thin tail. She expressed deep concern over her poems, which have, for many years now, been incorrectly attributed to a certain "Anonymous."

"It's an unfortunate typographical error," she wrote. "It happened many years ago, when I was just beginning my writing career. A careless publisher printed one of my first poems, and they accidentally misspelled my name. Despite all my letters to them, the mistake stood. Soon other firms began making the same error, and although I was grateful to them for publishing my little verses, I was a bit perturbed that they continued to ignore my countless requests to set the record straight. I can't say for certain, but it may have something to do with my being so small…hardly anyone takes a mouse seriously."

She went on to say that she had read much of my work and was quite fond of it. It occurred to her that I might be the very person to solve her predicament. "Surely the publishers will listen to *you*!" she wrote.

I immediately dashed off a reply to Ms. Mouse. "Yes! Publishers *do* occasionally misspell names…it's happened to me, too," I told her. We began a regular correspondence that continues to this day, in which we agreed that it was high time she had a book of her own, with her name spelled correctly. *Poems of A. Nonny Mouse* is the result.

I must add that Ms. Mouse was extremely grateful for my efforts on her behalf and kindly suggested that I include several of my own poems in this collection. I have written four and have placed them randomly throughout the book, without identification. If you are a good literary detective, you might be able to find them!

JACK PRELUTSKY
Albuquerque, New Mexico
1989

"Bubble," said the kettle,
"Bubble," said the pot.
"Bubble, bubble, bubble,
We are getting very hot!"

Shall I take you off the fire?
"No, you need not trouble.
This is just the way we talk—
Bubble, bubble, bubble!"

Jack Hall,
He is so small,
A mouse could eat him,
Hat and all.

Baby and I
Were baked in a pie,
The gravy was wonderful hot.
We had nothing to pay
To the baker that day,
And so we crept out of the pot.

I had a little brother
No bigger than my thumb.
I put him in the coffeepot—
He rattled like a drum.

The sausage is a cunning bird
With feathers long and wavy.
It swims about the frying pan
And makes its nest in gravy.

One day a boy went walking
And went into a store.
He bought a pound of sausages
And laid them on the floor.

The boy began to whistle
A merry little tune—
And all the little sausages
Danced around the room!

My father owns the butcher shop,
My mother cuts the meat,
And I'm the little hot dog
That runs around the street.

Get up, get up, you lazy head,
Get up, you lazy sinner.
We need those sheets for tablecloths,
It's nearly time for dinner!

That's the way to the zoo,
That's the way to the zoo—
The monkey house is nearly full,
But there's room enough for you.

My shoes are new and squeaky shoes,
They're very shiny, creaky shoes.
I wish I had my leaky shoes
That mother threw away.

I liked my old brown leaky shoes
Much better than these creaky shoes—
These shiny, creaky, squeaky shoes
I've got to wear today.

I love you, I love you,
I love you divine.
Please give me your bubblegum,
You're *sitting* on mine!

An Eskimo sleeps in his white bearskin
And sleeps rather well, I'm told.
Last night I slept in my little bare skin
And caught a terrible cold.

Mary had a little bear
To which she was so kind
That everywhere that Mary went
You saw her bear behind!

Fuzzy Wuzzy was a bear,
Fuzzy Wuzzy had no hair.
Fuzzy Wuzzy wasn't fuzzy,
Was he?

There was a young lady of Niger
Who smiled as she rode on a tiger.
They returned from the ride
With the lady inside—
And the smile on the face of the tiger.

Algy met a bear,
A bear met Algy.
The bear was bulgy,
The bulge was Algy.

As I was walking round the lake,
I met a little rattlesnake.
I gave him so much ice-cream cake,
It made his little belly ache.

If you should meet a crocodile,
Don't take a stick and poke him.
Ignore the welcome in his smile,
Be careful not to stroke him.
For as he sleeps upon the Nile,
He thinner gets and thinner.
And whene'er you meet a crocodile,
He's ready for his dinner.

A froggie sat on a lily pad,
Looking up at the sky.
The lily pad broke and the frog fell in,
Water all in his eye.

Froggy Boggy
tried to jump
on a stone
and got a bump.

It made his eyes
wink and frown
and turned his nose
upside down.

A centipede was happy quite,
Until a frog in fun
said, "Pray, which leg comes after which?"
This raised her mind to such a pitch,
She lay distracted in the ditch,
Considering how to run.

She fell into the bathtub,
She fell into the sink,
She fell into the raspberry jam
And
    came
        out
            pink.

There was a young lady of Crete
Who was so exceedingly neat,
    When she got out of bed,
    She stood on her head
To make sure of not soiling her feet.

As I went out
The other day,
My head fell off
and rolled away.

But when I noticed
It was gone,
I picked it up
And put it on.

A silly young fellow named Ben
Swallowed his wrist watch, and then
　　He coughed up the date
　　And the time on his plate—
April first, twenty seconds past ten.

Fatty, fatty, boom-a-latty—
　　This is the way he goes!
He is so large around the waist,
　　He cannot see his toes.

This is Mr. Skinny Linny—
　　See his long, lean face!
Instead of a regular suit of clothes
　　He wears an umbrella case!

I wish I was a little grub
With whiskers round my tummy.
I'd climb into a honeypot
And make my tummy gummy,
And then I'd crawl all over you
And make your tummy gummy too.

The fly made a visit to the grocery store.
Didn't even knock—went right in the door.
He took a bite of sugar and a bite of ham,
Then he sat down to rest on the grocery man.

Five tiny green peas, lying in a row
Inside a small green pod, one day began to grow.
They grew and they grew and they didn't stop
Until one day their pod went POP!

Curious fly,
Vinegar jug,
Slippery edge,
Pickled bug.

Little Arabella Miller
Found a woolly caterpillar.
First it crawled upon her mother,
Then upon her baby brother.
All said, "Arabella Miller,
Take away that caterpillar!"

A peanut sat on a railroad track,
His heart was all aflutter.
The five fifteen came rushing by—
Toot! Toot! Peanut butter!

There was a man—now please take note—
There was a man who had a goat.
He loved that goat—indeed he did—
He loved that goat just like a kid.

One day that goat felt frisk and fine,
Ate three red shirts from off the line.
The man, he grabbed him by the back
And tied him to a railroad track.

But when the train drove into sight,
That goat grew pale and green with fright.
He heaved a sigh as if in pain,
Coughed up those shirts, and flagged the train.

Oh, the funniest thing I've ever seen
Was a tomcat sewing on a sewing machine.
Oh, the sewing machine got running too slow,
And it took seven stitches in the tomcat's toe.

There's music in a hammer,
There's music in a nail,
There's music in a pussycat
When you step upon her tail.

The elephant goes like this and
   That,
He's terribly big and terribly
   Fat.
He has no fingers, he has no
   Toes,
But goodness gracious, what a
   Nose!

I'm SORRY

Way down South, where bananas grow,
A grasshopper stepped on an elephant's toe.
The elephant said with tears in his eyes,
"Pick on somebody your own size."

I dribbled catsup on my pet,
And that is why my cat's upset.

Betty Botter bought some butter,
"But," she said, "the butter's bitter.
If I put it in my batter,
It will make my batter bitter.
But a bit of better butter,
That would make my batter better."
So she bought a bit of butter
Better than her bitter butter,
And she put it in her batter
And the batter was not bitter.
So 'twas better Betty Botter
Bought a bit of better butter.

Through the teeth
And past the gums—
Look out, stomach,
Here it comes!

There was an old woman of Ryde
Who ate some green apples and died.
    Inside the lamented
    The apples fermented,
Making cider inside 'er inside.

Mary had a little lamb,
A lobster, and some prunes,
A glass of milk, a piece of pie,
And then some macaroons.

It made the busy waiters grin
To see her order so,
And when they carried Mary out,
Her face was white as snow.

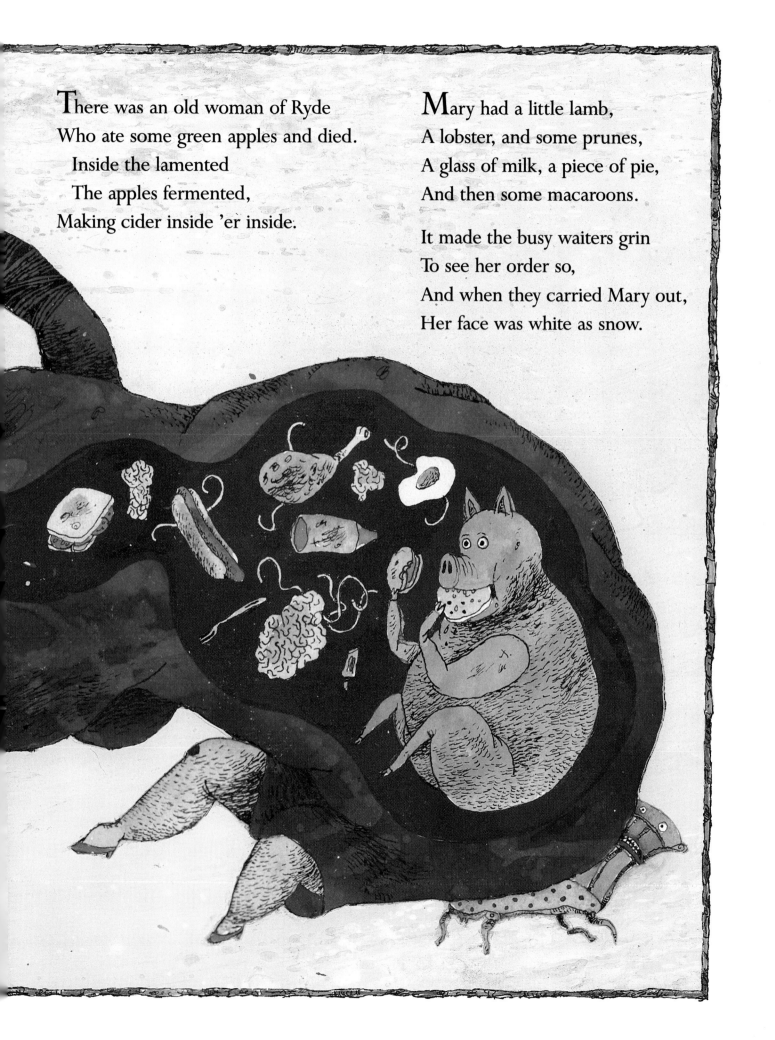

There was a small maiden named Maggie
Whose dog was enormous and shaggy.
   The front end of him
   Looked vicious and grim—
But the tail end was friendly and waggy.

There was a young man of Bengal
Who went to a fancy-dress ball.
   He went just for fun
   Dressed up as a bun—
And a dog ate him up in the hall.

I've got a dog as thin as a rail,
He's got fleas all over his tail.
Every time his tail goes flop,
The fleas on the bottom all hop to the top.

There was a little dog and he had a little tail,
And he used to wag, wag, wag it!
But when he was sad because he'd been bad,
On the ground he would drag, drag, drag it!

A very wise bird with a very long beak
Sat solemnly blinking away.
When asked why it was that he never would speak,
He replied, "I have nothing to say."

A clever gorilla named Gus
Drives a large cross-country bus.
When the passengers squeal,
"There's an ape at the wheel!"
He replies, "Leave the driving to us!"

Three young rats with black felt hats,
Three young ducks with white straw flats,
Three young dogs with curling tails,
Three young cats with demiveils,
Went out to walk with two young pigs
In satin vests and sorrel wigs,
But suddenly it changed to rain,
And so they all went home again.

Behold the wonders of the mighty deep,
Where crabs and lobsters learn to creep,
And little fishes learn to swim,
And clumsy sailors tumble in.

When a jolly young fisher named Fisher
Went fishing for fish in a fissure,
A fish, with a grin,
Pulled the fisherman in—
Now they're fishing the fissure for Fisher.

A sea serpent saw a big tanker,
Bit a hole in her side, and then sank her.
    It swallowed the crew
    In a minute or two—
And then picked its teeth with the anchor.

Little Johnny fished all day,
Fishes would not come his way.
"Had enough of this," said he,
"I'll be going home to tea!"
When the fishes saw him go,
Up they came all in a row,
Jumped about, and laughed with glee,
Shouting, "Johnny's gone to tea!"

Boots have tongues
But cannot talk.
Chairs have legs
But cannot walk.
Needles have eyes
But cannot see.
This chair has arms—
But it can't hug me!

TONGUE

TWISTER

How much wood would a woodchuck chuck
If a woodchuck could chuck wood?
He would chuck as much wood as a woodchuck would chuck
If a woodchuck could chuck wood.

Doctor Bell fell down the well
And broke his collarbone.
Doctors should attend the sick
And leave the well alone.

DOCTOR BELL

"Go, my son, and shut the shutter."
This I heard a mother utter.
"Shutter's shut," the boy did mutter.
"I can't shut 'er any shutter."

CELIA

Celia sat beside the seaside,
Quite beside herself was she.
For beside her on the leeside
No one sat beside her, see?

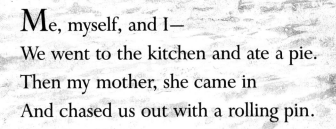

Me, myself, and I—
We went to the kitchen and ate a pie.
Then my mother, she came in
And chased us out with a rolling pin.

PAST president

Now I lay me down to rest,
I pray I pass tomorrow's test.
If I should die before I wake,
That's one less test I'll have to take.

I wish you'd speak when you're spoken to,
I wish you'd do as you're bid.
I wish you'd shut the door after you,
I wish you'd be a good kid!

I often pause and wonder
At fate's peculiar ways.
For nearly all our famous men
Were born on holidays.

The Man in the Moon as he sails the sky
Is a very remarkable skipper,
But he made a mistake when he tried to take
A drink of milk from the Dipper.
He dipped right out of the Milky Way
And slowly and carefully filled it.
The Big Bear growled and the Little Bear howled,
And frightened him so that he spilled it!

The firefly is a funny bug,
He hasn't any mind.
He blunders all the way through life
With his headlight on behind.

They strolled down the lane together,
The sky was studded with stars.
They reached the gate in silence,
And he lifted down the bars.
She neither smiled nor thanked him,
Because she knew not how.
For he was just a farmer's boy
and she a Jersey cow.

The farm is in a flurry,
The rooster's caught the flu—
His cock-a-doodle-doo has changed
To cock-a-doodle-chooooooo!

The barnyard fowls that lay our eggs
Have pointed beaks and scaly legs,
But some, which are considered freaks,
Have pointed legs and scaly beaks.

Coo, coo, coo!
It's as much as a pigeon
 Can do
To bring up two!
But the little wren
 Can manage ten
And bring them up
 Like gentlemen!

The codfish lays ten thousand eggs,
 The homely hen lays one.
The codfish never cackles
 To tell you what she's done.
And so we scorn the codfish
 While the humble hen we prize,
Which only goes to show you
 That it pays to advertise.

It's hard to lose a friend
When your heart is full of hope,
But it's worse to lose a towel
When your eyes are full of soap.

Jolly Roger lived up a tree,
You climbed there by a rope.
I'd often go for a cup of tea,
Which he brewed up with some soap.

Once I found a sock in mine,
It made me wince a bit.
But Roger told me, "Never mind.
It's old and doesn't fit."

Don't worry if your job is small
And your rewards are few.
Remember that the mighty oak
Was once a nut like you.